GEOFFREY GETS THE JITTERS

For Noah

Some other books by Nadia Shireen

Barbara Throws a Wobbler
Billy and the Pirates
Billy and the Beast
Billy and the Dragon
The Bumblebear
The Cow Who Fell to Earth
Good Little Wolf
Hey, Presto!
Yeti and the Bird

PUFFIN BOOKS

UK | USA | Canada | Ireland | Australia | India | New Zealand | South Africa

Puffin Books is part of the Penguin Random House group of companies
whose addresses can be found at global.penguinrandomhouse.com.

www.penguin.co.uk   www.puffin.co.uk   www.ladybird.co.uk

Penguin
Random House
UK

First published 2023

001

Copyright © Nadia Shireen, 2023

The moral right of the author/illustrator has been asserted

Printed in Spain

A CIP catalogue record for this book is available from the British Library

ISBN: 978–0–241–62368–8

All correspondence to:
Puffin Books, Penguin Random House Children's,
One Embassy Gardens, 8 Viaduct Gardens, London SW11 7BW

MIX
Paper | Supporting
responsible forestry
FSC® C018179

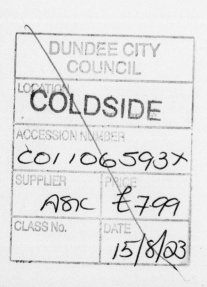

GEOFFREY GETS THE JITTERS

NADIA SHIREEN

PUFFIN

This is Geoffrey.

If you asked Geoffrey if he were OK, he would say,

But Geoffrey is *not* OK.

He hasn't been feeling
quite right for some time.

It had started last night
as he lay in bed.

Geoffrey was thinking about the next day.

He was
looking forward to
seeing Barbara.

He knew there would
be pizza for lunch.

But what was happening
after lunch?
Geoffrey couldn't remember.

Suddenly, he had felt a
peculiar flutter in his tummy.
A tiny little jitter.

And then he thought . . .

What if Barbara
didn't like him
anymore?

What if he *lost* Big Dave?

What if . . .

...massive dinosaurs with lasers coming out of their eyes **STOMPED** all over him?

It was all *quite* worrying.

Geoffrey's tummy had been feeling jittery ever since.

It was as if his tummy
was full of **wiggly worms.**

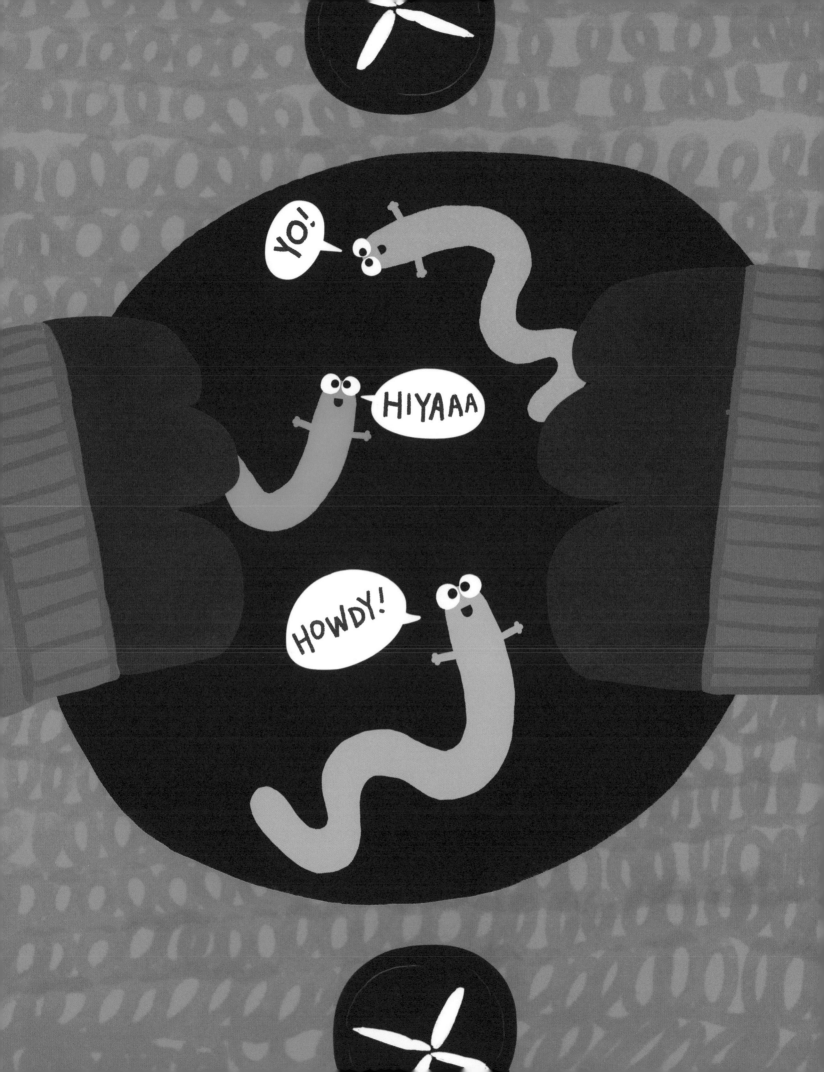

Then Geoffrey started to feel all hot and sweaty.

Everything suddenly seemed *too*

BRIGHT

and *too* NOISY.

NOISY NOISY

NOISY NOISY

By now, the jitters felt *really* out of control.

All Geoffrey wanted to do was hide.

So he did.

But it turned out that there was
no hiding from his jitters.

"Excuse me," said Geoffrey.
"But who are you and what are you doing?"

"Hiya! We're your jitters," said a jitter.

"Why have I got jitters?" asked Geoffrey.

"You must be worrying about something," said the jitter.

"Whenever you get really worried about something, that's when you get a jitter."

"But why are there so many of you?" asked Geoffrey.

OH, IF THERE'S ONE JITTER...
...SOON THERE'LL BE ANOTHER
AND ANOTHER
AND ANOTHER!

Now, the jitters had completely taken over.
Geoffrey decided he'd had enough.

"How do I get rid of you?"
he asked.

"Oh, that's easy,"
said a helpful jitter.
"Take a deeeeeep breath in . . .

. . . and slooooowly blow out the birthday candles
of a *very* old tortoise."

"Then stretch up to the sky . . .

and down to your toes –

we *really* hate that."

Geoffrey started to feel a little better. So . . .

... he decided he needed to get hold of a jitter for himself!

Then he could take **a *really* good look** at it.

GOTCHA!

Well, the jitter didn't like that *at all*.

"Oh!" said Geoffrey. "So *that's* what I've been worrying about."

"Don't tell anyone," said the jitter. "Or else I'll completely disappear."

So Geoffrey stepped
outside into the sunshine
and saw his friend, Barbara.

"Hey, Geoffrey," said Barbara. "How are you?"

"Well, I have these worries," said Geoffrey.

And now, Geoffrey **really** *was* OK.

WORRIES
(A Very Useful Guide)

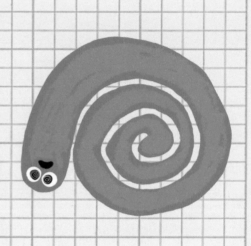

fig.1: The Brood
Something happened a long time ago, but the Brood is still thinking about it.

fig.2: The Niggle
Every now and then the Niggle will poke you with a tiny stick and remind you about something annoying.

fig.3: The Spiral
When one worry links to another worry and then another worry and soon you are spinning, aaargh!

fig.4: The Frazzle
Look, the Frazzle is very busy and can't stop. Stressed? NO, THEY ARE FINE.

fig.5: The Fret
(Doesn't want to talk about it and is going to hide under a blanket.)

fig.6: The Panic
Has lost control! Is going to run around screaming! Is wearing pants on its head!